JAMAL
JEALOUSAURUS

Published in paperback in 2015 by
Wayland

Wayland
338 Euston Road
London NW1 3BH

Wayland Australia
Level 17/207 Kent Street
Sydney, NSW 2000

Senior editor: Victoria Brooker
Creative design: Basement68
Digital colour: Molly Hahn

British Library Cataloguing
in Publication Data:

Moses, Brian, 1950-
   Jamal Jealousaurus. --
   (Dinosaurs have feelings, too)
   1. Children's stories--Pictorial
   works.
   I. Title II. Series III. Gordon, Mike,
   1948 Mar. 16-
   823.9'2-dc23
ISBN: 9780750280228

Printed in China
10 9 8 7 6 5 4 3 2 1

Wayland is a division of
Hachette Children's Books,
an Hachette UK company.
www.hachette.co.uk

JAMAL
JEALOUSAURUS

Written by
Brian Moses

Illustrated by
Mike Gordon

WAYLAND

Jamal was a green-eyed jealousaurus.

The more jealous he became, the brighter his eyes shone.

He was jealous of his
brother's skill at games.

"I wish I could beat him
at Swamp Escape."

8

He was jealous of his friends on their fast new Bronto-bikes when he only had a scooter.

He was jealous of his cousins who always seemed to have far more holidays than he did.

11

Jamal decided to tell his mum
how jealous he felt.

She said, "It's natural to feel a little bit jealous, but we all have to learn how to deal with it."

"I'm a bit jealous of the dinosaur next door," his mum explained.

"She has a much bigger cave than we do, and she's always buying new things."

"And I'm jealous of my friend's new dinocar," said his dad.

"It's such a smooth drive and it doesn't bounce over the boulders like our car does."

"But sometimes I get so jealous, it feels like slimy creepers are crawling up from my toes and curling round my tummy until I can't think of anything else."

"I hate it when I feel like that," he said.

"You've got to remember all the good things that you can do," said Jamal's dad. "Think about how clever you are at tailball."

"Maybe one day you'll play for
Dinosaur United against the Jurassic Giants."

"And when you feel jealous, you need
to think of all the good things you have,"
Jamal's mum told him.

"Think of that special holiday we had last year when we went to 'Adventure Island'."

"Remember also, Jamal, that other dinosaurs might be jealous of you."

"You mean jealous of my boneboarding skills," replied Jamal, with a grin.

Every day now, Jamal tries his hardest not to be too jealous.

"Maybe I can be a 'Notsojealousaurus' or an 'Onlyalittlebitjealousaurus.'"

You can always tell how successful
he is by looking into his eyes.

He's doing well today, can you see why?

NOTES FOR PARENTS AND TEACHERS

Read the book with children either individually or in groups.
Talk to them about what makes them jealous. How do they feel
when they are jealous? Do they recognise any of the things that
make Jamal jealous?

Children won't always understand that feelings of anger
and frustration are often part of jealousy. You could help them to
make masks that show, what they feel is, a jealous expression. Now
talk about the expressions they put on their masks.

Help children to compose short poems that focus on their
own jealous feelings:

> I feel jealous when my brother wins a prize and I don't.
> I feel jealous when my teacher says how good my friend's
>   reading is, but doesn't praise me.
> I feel jealous when I see other children with electronic
>   games that I wanted for Christmas.
> I feel jealous...

Can children offer suggestions as to how these jealous
feelings can be overcome?

Jamal's parents remind Jamal that others might be jealous of the
skills that he has. Jamal then thinks of his 'boneboarding skills'.

Ask children to think of things that they are good at. Would others be jealous of their skills?

Some children may like to write stories that focus on one of the scenes from pages 6 to 11. Will their stories have a positive or negative outcome? Talk to them about what they have written and why they decided to write what they did.

Ask children to think about why adults might get jealous.

Mum's jealous of her sister's new boots. She'd like a pair like that.
Dad's jealous of our neighbour's new television. It's got such
a huge screen.
Our Nan's jealous of all the things we have to play with these
days. "I didn't have much at all when I was young," she says.

Have fun with ideas about jealousy too – what would the dog be jealous of, or the cat, or a spider, or a rabbit?

Our dog is jealous of the dog next door and his
new ball. He'd like to take it home with him.
Our cat is jealous of another cat's singing. If only
he could howl like she can.

Explore the notion of jealousy further through the sharing of picture books mentioned in the book list on page 32.

BOOKS TO SHARE

I Have Feelings by Jana Novotny Hunter, illustrated by
Sue Porter (Frances Lincoln)
Explores a whole range of feelings including jealous ones.
Small children will love the little star of the book.

Lulu & the Birthday Party by Belinda Hollyer, illustrated by
Emma Damon (Frances Lincoln)
Lulu gets very jealous as her brother Billy's birthday approaches.
A story about childhood jealousy and sibling rivalry.

Rosie's Babies by Martin Waddell, illustrated by
Penny Dale (Walker Books)
Four year old Rosie is just a little jealous of the new baby who
seems to have all Mum's attention at the moment.

Katie Morag & the Two Grandmothers by
Mairi Hedderwick (Red Fox)
Even adults experience feelings of jealousy.

I Feel Jealous by Brian Moses,
illustrated by Mike Gordon (Wayland)
Looking at childhood jealousy in
an amusing yet reassuring way.